Licensed exclusively to Top That Publishing Ltd
Tide Mill Way, Woodbridge, Suffolk, IP12 1AP, UK
www.topthatpublishing.com
Text copyright © 2010 Nicole Snitselaar
Illustration copyright © 2010 Coralie Saudo
All rights reserved
2 4 6 8 9 7 5 3 1
Manufactured in China

Written by Nicole Snitselaar
Illustrated by Coralie Saudo

ISBN 978-1-84956-073-3

A catalogue record for this book is available from the British Library

# Hiku

by
Nicole Snitselaar and Coralie Saudo

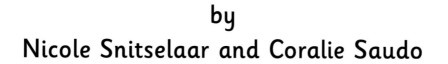

Hiku, a little penguin, was feeling grumpy one morning.

It was one of those days, when the ice was too bright,
the sun was too hot, and his mummy woke him up too early.
'Don't forget that all of our family are visiting today!'
she reminded him.

Oh no! A family visit was the last thing Hiku wanted!
Smiling, greeting, being polite and listening to,
'You look so cute with your white heart-shaped tummy!' all day.
Or having everyone sing, 'Hiku, Hiku, say cheese or you'll freeze!'
Why had he been given such a silly name!
'I want to be alone,' grumbled Hiku.

Hiku !

Hiku !

Hiku !

Soon, Hiku saw his family arriving, some by sea, some over the ice field. Hiku slipped past without being noticed and waddled to his hiding place. 'At last!' he whispered with relief, snuggling into his special snow hole.

'It's so nice to have some peace and quiet,' thought Hiku.
But, very soon he grew bored and lonely.
Sitting in his hiding place, Hiku started to think of some
happy times that he had spent with his family.

That wonderful day at the swimming pool ...
sliding, playing, splashing, getting soaked!

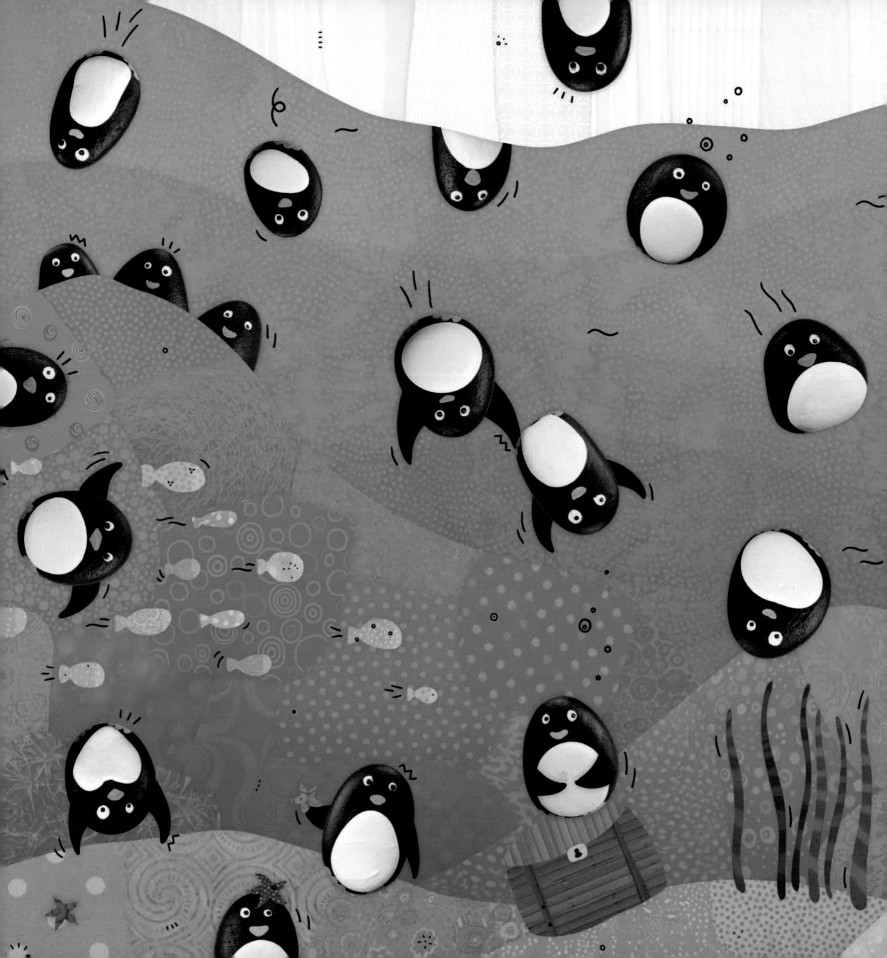

Diving deep underwater,
searching for lost treasures.

All the fun and laughter of playing hide-and-seek.

Climbing and performing acrobatics at the adventure park.

That time, when full of wonder,
Hiku and his family huddled together,
watching the Southern Lights.

And those evenings in front of the blazing fire ...

grilling fish and listening to scary stories.

'Oh, what fun my family and I have together,' sighed Hiku.
'What am I doing here all by myself?
I hope it's not too late ...'
And, without a second thought, Hiku waddled back to join his family.

Hiku arrived just in time for the family photo!

'Ready? 1, 2, 3 … Hiku!' said the photographer.
'Hiku, Hiku, say cheese or you'll freeze!' laughed everyone.
'A name that makes your family smile isn't that bad!' thought Hiku,
and he joined in with the family fun and games.

Say goodbye, Hiku.